Plant a Rose

Helen Turnbull Phelps

She who stoops to plant a rose—
Whose fragrance wafts toward the sky—
Plants splendor not for self alone,
But shares with strangers passing by.

She who plants a rose plants friends,
Unknowingly though it may be.
The language of the blossoms weaves
A mystic spell of harmony.

For those who pause beside the bush
And share her smile across a rose,
Cannot but feel that gentle tug
As budding friendship grows and grows.

For smiles across a garden wall
Are strangely somehow richly blessed,
By language only flowers know . . .
And roses seem to speak it best!

Photo Opposite
Cascading Roses
Larry Lefever/Grant Heilman Photography, Inc.

PRELUDE

Jean Frances Zyats

I saw a flower born today
        And watched with fascination
While unseen hands began to open
        This miniature creation.

It stretched its petals sleepily,
        Reluctantly unfurled,
Then opened wide its upturned arms
        To greet the waiting world.

Swallowtail Butterfly on Pink Iris
Ina Mackey

PURPLE IRIS

Theresa E. Black

We thinned the rows, for they had grown
And vastly multiplied.
Unwanted extra bulbs were thrown
Away or cast aside.
We left them there for lack of room
And now they shame our faces . . .
For regal purple iris bloom
In unaccustomed places.

WHO LOOKS AT BEAUTY

Grace Noll Crowell

Who looks at beauty with glad eyes
And finds in it surcease from care,
Who marks each small and lovely thing,
Is praising God all unaware.

Whose heart lifts up in gratitude
For cloud and leaf and budding stem,
Is sharing the delight he knew
The morning he created them.

Whose ears are keened to catch the first
Faint bird note in the darkened trees,
Can hear the music of the spheres,
The ageless heavenly symphonies.

Who holds his breath at the far scent
Of some wild blossom on the air,
Is giving thanks unknowingly,
Is voicing an unspoken prayer.

WHO HATH A GARDEN

Thomas Curtis Clark

Who hath a garden—he has joy,
However small his plot may be.
Far his horizons; in his estate,
Master of beauty and life is he.

God has graciously smiled on him,
Made him a helper in his great task—
Building a glorious world in time—
What finer work could anyone ask?

Who hath a garden—he has friends.
Lilies and roses will not forsake;
When they depart, 'tis but for a time,
They will return when the spring
    winds wake.

Let him rejoice on his kingly throne—
Who hath a garden of pink and gold.
Kings bear burdens and soon are gray,
Who hath a garden shall not grow old.

Photo Opposite
English-style Garden
Larry Lefever/Grant Heilman Photography, Inc.

MAY

Marjorie Martin

Allow me to hold May to my heart,
This delightful month of blooming flowers
And birdsong that awakens me
With drifting melody for hours.

The greenest month of all the year
Comes to an end too soon,
But leaves rainbow flowers everywhere
As a welcome in, to June.

Photo Overleaf
Mustard and Lupine
Redwood National Park, California
Jeff Gnass Photography

Photo Opposite
Chinese Wisteria
Lefever/Grishow from
Grant Heilman Photography, Inc.

CHOCOLATE & COMPANY

Chocolate Peach Shortcake

2 eggs, separated
¼ cup sugar
¼ cup unsifted all-purpose flour
3 tablespoons HERSHEY'S Cocoa
2 tablespoons sugar
¼ teaspoon baking soda
3 tablespoons water
2 tablespoons sugar
1 cup heavy or whipping cream
⅓ cup confectioners' sugar
½ teaspoon vanilla
2 cups (16-ounce can) sliced peaches, well drained

Grease bottom of 9-inch square pan; line with wax paper and grease paper. Beat 2 egg yolks 3 minutes on medium speed. Gradually add ½ cup sugar; continue beating 2 minutes. Combine flour, HERSHEY'S Cocoa, 2 tablespoons sugar and the baking soda; add alternately with water on low speed just until batter is smooth. Beat egg whites until foamy; add 2 tablespoons sugar, and beat until stiff peaks form. Carefully fold beaten egg whites into chocolate mixture. Spread batter evenly into prepared pan. Bake at 375° for 12 to 14 minutes or until top springs back when touched lightly. Cool 10 minutes; remove from pan and remove wax paper. Cool completely; chill while preparing filling.

Beat cream, confectioners' sugar and vanilla in large mixer bowl until stiff. Cut cake layer in half horizontally. Place 1 cake layer upside-down on serving plate; frost with about 1 cup whipped cream. With decorator's tube or spoon, make a ring of whipped cream ½ inch high and 1 inch wide around edge of layer. Fill center with peach slices for top of cake. Carefully place second layer, top side up, on filling. Gently spread whipped cream on top of cake. With decorator's tube or spoon, make border of whipped cream around edge of top layer of cake. Arrange remaining peach slices in center. Chill before serving.

Recipe and photo courtesy of
HERSHEY FOODS CORPORATION

PATENT LEATHER OXFORDS

While in the store recently, I watched a small child with a very bored expression on her little face choosing three pairs of shoes in varied colors. Her well-dressed, preoccupied mother sat next to her on the edge of the chair, alternately looking at her watch and urging the child to make up her mind. The child obliged, and the pair left the store hurriedly, the mother carrying three boxes and her daughter running behind, both appearing relieved that another tiresome task had been accomplished.

Watching them took me back to a memorable Saturday night when, as child of six, I received my first pair of black patent leather oxfords. It also made me realize that affluence can cause loss rather than gain, and that having more is not the guaranteed path to pleasure and fulfillment.

My widowed mother raised her five children in a small town in the Midwest. We were what was considered a poor family, although I cannot remember any unhappiness or discontent.

The main street of our town was a block long, with stores on either side. Saturday was the only night of the week that the stores were open. This was not just the end of the work week, it was a community event. The streets were brightly lit and filled with people of all ages. The women shopped for groceries and other goods for the home, met their friends, and chatted; the men stood in groups, discussing the weather or crops; and the children darted in and out among them. We spent the evening running up one side of the street and down the other, going in and out of the stores and pressing our faces against the windows to admire the displays inside.

It was on one such night that I first saw the patent leather oxfords; from then on, I noticed little else.

In our family, we each had one pair of shoes at a time and we knew they would not be replaced until the soles and heels were completely beyond repair. At the time I saw the oxfords in the window, my high-topped ones were wearing thin, and I knew that because I was due to start school that year, they would have to be replaced. When I showed the oxfords to my older sister, her remark was, "Well, they're patent leather and you know that cracks, so they wouldn't last long enough."

Disappointing as her opinion was, I understood it very well, as this was a familiar phrase to all of us, used again and again about anything we played with, ate, or wore. Our weekly nickel, which we spent on Saturday night, always lay in our pockets, heavy but secure, until nearly time for the stores to dim their lights. We were "making it last." How to spend it was a mouth-watering decision, and whatever we purchased—usually an ice cream cone in the summer—we kept this thought in mind. We would watch each other out of the corners of our eyes and, when my sister licked her ice cream, I would lick mine. By cautiously watching each other, we usually popped the last end of the crisp cone into our mouths at exactly the same time. Thus, we not only "made it last," but we also came out even, so that neither of us had to envy the other the last tasty mouthful.

For several successive Saturday nights I stood in front of the window of the general store admiring my shoes, oblivious to my friends running up and down the street behind me. After what my sister had told me, I felt sure that the shoes were unattainable and I never even mentioned them to my mother. But still, I stared and dreamed of my feet encased in their shining smoothness.

Then the night came when Mother said, "Tonight, we must go and get your new school shoes."

We went into the general store hand in hand, and I sat down to wait my turn. When I heard Mother tell the clerk, "We would like to see a pair of the black patent leather oxfords in the window," I shivered in anticipation. When they were put on my feet, I could hardly stand on my trembling legs, ankles cool and free of the restricting leather and laces of my old high-topped shoes.

Still, feeling I must warn her, I said to Mother, "But Winnie says they crack and won't last."

Mother smiled, squeezed my hand, and answered, "We'll just take them anyway."

I left the store, both arms wrapped around the shoe box, cradling it like a baby close to my heart. My night was complete. Every few steps I smiled up at Mother until she burst out laughing and asked, "Did you think I didn't know what you were looking at in that window every Saturday night?" She put her arm around my shoulders, pulling me so close that I felt her long skirt swish against my legs the rest of the way home.

Before going to sleep, I removed the shoes from the box and placed them on top of the old sewing machine just opposite my bed. I wanted them to be the first thing I saw when I opened my eyes Sunday morning. It took quite a while to arrange them, as I couldn't decide whether to have the shiny toes facing me, or to have them sideways so that I could see all of them at one glance. Finally they were placed to my satisfaction and I snuggled under my patchwork quilt and looked at them until all the lights were out.

I do not recall now if they "lasted," but I am sure that no precious jewel has ever shone more brightly or made anyone happier than did those shoes shining softly in the sun when I opened my eyes the next morning.

Elinore Haglund

HER MOTHER

Alice Cary

Oh, if I could only make you see
   The clear blue eyes, the tender smile,
The sovereign sweetness, the gentle grace,
The woman's soul, the angel's face
   That are beaming on me all the while,
I need not speak these foolish words
Yet one word tells you all I would say—
She is my mother: you will agree
That all the rest may be thrown away.

Photo Opposite
Remembrances
Al Riccio

SHE WORE IT WELL

Caroline Eyring Miner

She loved the sunset with flaming plumes;
She loved the quiet of shady rooms.
She saw in every person she met,
Someone generous, kind; I shan't forget
Her loving hand on a tousled head,
Her earnest prayer for the unsung dead.
She loved to work and arose at dawn
And counted the hours
  by the tasks she had done.
And every day she wanted to know
Someone was better able to go
Along his way and carry his load
Because she'd cheered him along the road.
She made a religion of happiness;
She wore it well—like a golden dress.

22

REFLECTIONS

Robert James Ryan

I sometimes look into my mother's eyes,
And witness past and present meeting;
Apprehension for the unseen future;
And sorrow for all things fleeting.

In old photographs I have seen
A young miss in fashion of the day.
How clear the beauty of your youth,
Eyes smiling in memories now far away.

A lifetime of love-filled deeds
I glimpse now in a well of tears,
And see beauty set in each line of care
That has formed over each of my years.

No beauty of youth is lost for you,
But has grown over all of your time.
Come, see in my eyes how you are today,
O beautiful mother of mine.

SWEET MEMORIES

Caroline Eyring Miner

Sweet memories like scented flowers now
Bring back your sacred presence once again.
And I can feel your cool hand on my brow
As I was wont to in my childhood when
A fever raged. At sunset when the sky
Is golden, I can hear you say, "Take note
How gold shames garish red, and ever try
To be demure and modest." Once you wrote
Above my mirror so I'd surely see,
"Be true to self, my daughter; you will find
Respect from others starts with you." Your knee
Became my altar where I learned the kind
Of faith that opens hidden doors for me
Leading to peace unto eternity.

Dolley Madison: A Mother to Her Country

Jean Gwinnett

At dawn, on the morning of August 24, 1814, a lone figure stood atop the White House roof. Peering through a spyglass, Dolley Madison strained to catch a glimpse of her husband in the distance. James, the fourth president of the fledgling nation, was with his troops, however, trying to rally the poorly trained militia men. The situation was grim. The War of 1812 had strained the country for almost two years. Earlier that week, the British had landed a fleet carrying a raiding force of 4,500 veteran infantrymen. This force was now less than one day's march from Washington, D. C. As Dolley watched from the rooftop, she saw swarms of panicked citizens streaming out of the city. Wagons loaded with trunks and household goods choked the roads leading toward the Potomac as people fled to the safety of Virginia.

Yet Dolley stood firm; she was determined to give her husband and her nation an example of strength, courage, and leadership; as first lady, her role was that of symbolic mother to the country she loved, and she would not abandon that role in this crisis.

The daughter of Virginia patriots, Dolley moved with the family to Philadelphia at the age of fourteen. She was raised as a Quaker, and her parents instilled in her the ideals of equality, moral accountability, and charity. She married James Madison, who was seventeen years her senior and not a member of the Quaker faith, despite the disapproval of her parents and her religious community.

It was a courage born of love that enabled Dolley to endure the denouncements and rumors that accompanied this "defection from the faith," and it would be the same courageous love that would enable her to endure the political critics who directed their wrath at the nation's first couple. As the War of 1812 engulfed the nation, the Madisons were urged by friends to abandon the White House for safer lodgings. But Dolley would not go. No one was running Dolley Madison out of her own home without a fight!

And so it was, this August morning, that she stood sentinel on the roof. Ignoring the repeated messages to flee, she had, instead, packed up the President's papers and sent them off for safekeeping with a trusted friend.

As the morning wore on, Dolley could hear the roar of the cannons in the distance. She watched straggling groups of militiamen flee into the city, running before the well-armed British. Eventually, even the troops assigned to protect the White House deserted their posts. Still, Dolley felt a deep personal responsibility for the house, for her role as First Lady, and for the example she must set in that position. Instead of running in fear, she ordered the staff to prepare the President's supper, convinced that panic would best be met head on with purpose.

As she supervised the preparations, however, a pair of messengers appeared at the door. They carried a personal message from the President urging his wife to leave Washington at once.

She would recall later that her first inclination was to position cannons at the White House windows and her second to booby trap the front door with gunpowder. Realizing the futility of both, however, she decided upon a third plan and proceeded to carry as much of the White House with her as she could.

Dolley removed the crimson draperies from the Oval Office and packed them into a waiting carriage, followed by several valuable books, and the White House silverware. And then, the gold framed Gilbert Stuart portrait of George Washington caught her eye. "Take it down!" she ordered. But the heavy frame had been screwed to the wall and would not budge.

As the shouts of the retreating troops, the rumble of fleeing carriages, and the blast of cannons filled the air, Dolley ordered the men to break the frame and free the canvas. This done, she ran and picked up a copy of the Declaration of Independence and dashed out the door.

A few hours later, British troops set the deserted mansion on fire, toasting their conquest with wine set out by Dolley Madison for her husband.

Their victory was to be short-lived, however. The news of the British burning the White House, and the story of Dolley Madison's courageous rescue of the portrait and the Declaration of Independence, reached New York quickly and stirred American men and women into action on their country's behalf. Within a month, the tide began to turn against the British, and in five more months, a treaty of peace was signed.

While the restoration of the White House would take some time, the restoration of the nation's spirits had already begun. Dolley Madison's devotion and strength set an example for U. S. citizens and dramatically illustrated a truth that mothers have always known: It is not only those who go to war who win great battles, but also those who remain at home.

Photo Overleaf
Springtime at San Juan Islands, Washington
Ed Cooper Photo

KLEIN GRANDMA

Marilyn Kratz

We always called her "Klein Grandma"—German for "little grandma"—because she was barely five feet tall and seemed to shrink shorter and shorter as the hump on her back grew larger. She has been gone for over twenty-five years now, but I still remember her, and I miss her in so many ways.

I miss the security of her unconditional love. She always had time for me and made me feel special.

I miss the way she bustled about, and her graying, reddish hair wreathing her face in springy waves, held in place by a neat braided coil at the back of her neck. I can still picture the impish glint in her pale blue eyes whenever she grinned.

And, of course, I miss her wonderful cooking. In fact, many of my happiest childhood memories are focused around the big oval table in her sunny, lace-curtained dining room.

Grandma became an expert at creating meatless meals during her years as a struggling parent on the often drought-stricken southeastern South Dakota prairie. She cooked many a delicious and satisfying meal on her old cob-burning cookstove.

When she moved into town as a middle-aged widow, she had her sons set the old stove up in her basement, even though she had modern electrical appliances in her kitchen. She just knew her bread-dough dumplings would not turn out right unless she made them on that cookstove.

Nobody could make dumplings like those that Klein Grandma made. She tried to tell her daughters and daughters-in-law exactly how to do it, but theirs were never as fluffy or as crisply browned on the bottom. Perhaps the secret lay in knowing just how long to let them rise under the dish towel, or just how many potatoes to layer under them in the old dented aluminum roaster, or how to seal the roaster lid with a dampened rag while the dumplings steamed inside. Such things cannot be written on a recipe card.

Grandma loved to begin a big family meal with what seemed, in my little girl eyes, to be a "vat" of homemade chicken noodle soup. That would be followed by hearty main dishes; never fancy, but always satisfying. And then there came dessert!

I remember fluffy yellow cake with broiled icing and wonderful apple dumplings with their flaky pastry hiding half a cinnamon-spiced apple. Then there were her unforgettable sour cream cookies. They were huge, cakey cookies topped with brown sugar icing. After Klein Grandma died, I asked to see her recipe file so I could copy the recipe for those cookies, but it could not be found. I suspect she kept it in her head and never wrote it down.

My dear Klein Grandma was never rich or famous, but she left me the treasured memories of happy hours in her home, where she was always ready to share her love, or a dumpling or a cookie or two. The "flavor" she added to my life made us both richer in a special way. And even though we called her Klein Grandma, she will always be a big part of my life.

CRAFTWORKS

BREAD DOUGH HEARTS

Bread dough is a marvelous medium for people who like to work with clay. It is lighter and cleaner than many other types of modeling material, and has an attractive egg shell-like matte finish. These hearts can be made with readily available materials. Finished hearts can be displayed in a variety of ways: those in the photo opposite have been mounted on a wooden panel.

MATERIALS NEEDED:

    12 slices of bread
        white glue
    1   tube of white water-color
        liquid dish detergent
        Vaseline or cold cream
        rolling pin
        freezer paper
        nesting set of 3 or more heart shaped
          cookie cutters
        plastic straws, regular and cocktail size
        toothpicks
        paint brushes
        fine wire
        sharp kitchen knife or spoon
        water-base paints in colors of choice
        (tempura, acrylics, or tube water-colors)
        clear spray varnish or polyurethane
        display board and hooks (optional)

PREPARING THE DOUGH:

Step One—Remove crusts from bread. Tear into pieces in a mixing bowl. Add 6 tablespoons white glue, 1½ teaspoons white water color, and 1 teaspoon dish detergent. Mix well with a spoon. Apply cold cream or Vaseline to hands and knead well. Add more bread or glue as required to make dough smooth and workable. Put mixture in a plastic bag in refrigerator and let sit at least 1 hour.

Step Two—Roll out dough until about ¼ inch thick. Placing the dough on freezer paper, cut it with a heart shaped cutter at least 3 inches at the widest part. (Dough will shrink as it dries). Selecting the next smaller size cutter, carefully place it on the cut heart. Press gently to make the line for the outside border. Press the smallest cutter gently into the center of the heart to define the center.

Step Three—Pinch and indent at the end of a plastic straw so that it takes the shape of a tiny heart. Press it into the center of the plaque to make six tiny tulips or, for daisies, use the tip of a cocktail straw to make groups of four petals. Stems can be etched in with a knife or a toothpick.

With the tip of another straw, carefully decorate the middle panel with rows of scallop. Between the scallops you can make dots with a toothpick now, or wait and later make dots with the end of a toothpick dipped in paint. Be creative and work quickly while dough is moist.

Step Four—Insert a wire loop into the top of the heart for hanging. Turn the heart frequently as it dries to prevent warping.

Step Five—As soon as the plaque is dry enough to be handled easily, it is ready for painting. When the paint is completely dry, spray the heart with varnish or polyurethane.

Vanni Lowdenslager, a resident of Gunnison, Colorado, has been working with bread dough for several years, and her crafts have been featured in several national publications. In addition to hearts, she makes birds, flowers, and figurines out of bread dough.

Some Small Delight

Milly Walton

Give me this day some small delight,
Some simple joy to cheer my soul,
A singing bird upon the bough,
A drifting cloud in sky's blue bowl;
The pealing laughter of my child,
The glint of sunlight on his hair,

The feel of his warm hand in mine,
Of these dear things make me aware;
A blossom in the garden spot,
The music of the poplar trees,
The fragrance of a dew-washed earth,
What could enchant me more than these?
Grant me the perception that I may
Live deeply through this chartless day,
And when I go to sleep tonight
Be thankful for each small delight.

TODDLER LOGIC

I love my baby brother,
Mom brought him home today.
I'd like him even better
If he'd get up and play.

Mom says he can't eat our food,
Can't sit or stand or walk.
I feel so sorry for him,
For he can't even talk.

When Mom had told me all of this,
It made me real upset.
Why did they give him to us,
If he wasn't finished yet?

Edith M. Emmons
Mesa, Arizona

MOTHER

It must be part of God you see
When we look in a mother's eyes.
He must be living in her heart
To make her so gentle and so wise.

It must be he who helps her
Make it through each day.
To teach little children
Of loving and of play.

It must be he who gives her patience
Whenever they are bad.
It must be he who helps her comfort them
When they are hurt or sad.

And he will help her to realize
When her raising them is done,
That they are now no longer
Her little daughters or her little sons.

It is he who watches over them
When this world she must depart,
And he who keeps her memory fresh
In their minds and in their hearts.

Gloria J. Aylesworth
Bemidji, Minnesota

Reflections

"Good mornin' little girl,"
And she smiles her baby smile—
"I have come to see you
And love you for a while."

Tiny little fingers
Clutch my fingers too—
As I sing and rock and cuddle,
My day is full of you.

Days of caring, learning, sharing,
Each one like no other—
Those special, precious moments,
Between granddaughter and grandmother.

C. J. Ellefson
Buffalo, Minnesota

Editor's Note: Readers are invited to submit unpublished, original poetry, short anecdotes, and humorous reflections on life for possible publication in future *Ideals* issues. Please send copies only; manuscripts will not be returned. Writers receive $10 for each published submission. Send material to "Readers' Reflections," Ideals Publishing Corporation, P. O. Box 140300, Nashville, Tennessee, 37214-0300.

A SLICE OF LIFE

Edgar A. Guest

Where's Mamma?

Comes in flying from the street;
　　"Where's Mamma?"
Friend or stranger, thus he'll greet:
　　"Where's Mamma?"
Doesn't want to say hello,
Home from school or play he'll go
Straight to what he wants to know:
　　"Where's Mamma?"

Many times a day he'll shout,
　　"Where's Mamma?"
Seems afraid that she's gone out;
　　"Where's Mamma?"
Is his first thought at the door—
She's the one he's looking for,
And he questions o'er and o'er,
　　"Where's Mamma?"

Can't be happy till he knows:
　　"Where's Mamma?"
So he begs us to disclose
　　"Where's Mamma?"
And it often seems to me,
As I hear his anxious plea,
That no sweeter phrase can be:
　　"Where's Mamma?"

Like to hear it day by day;
　　"Where's Mamma?"
Loveliest phrase that lips can say:
　　"Where's Mamma?"
And I pray as time shall flow,
And the long years come and go,
That he'll always want to know
　　"Where's Mamma?"

Edgar A. Guest began his career in 1895 at the age of fourteen when his work first appeared in the Detroit Free Press. *His column was syndicated in over 300 newspapers, and he became known as "The Poet of the People."*

The Child's Wish in June

Caroline Gilman

Mother, mother, the winds are at play,
Prithee, let me be idle today.
Look, dear mother, the flowers all lie
Languidly under the bright blue sky.

See, how slowly the streamlet glides;
Look, how the violet roguishly hides;
Even the butterfly rests on the rose,
And scarcely sips the sweets as he goes.

Poor Tray is asleep in the noon-day sun,
And the flies go about him one by one;
And pussy sits near with a sleepy grace,
Without ever thinking of washing her face.

There flies a bird to a neighboring tree,
But very lazily flieth he,
And he sits and twitters a gentle note,
That scarcely ruffles his little throat.

You bid me be busy; but, mother, hear
How the hum-drum grasshopper soundeth near,
And the soft west wind is so light in its play,
It scarcely moves a leaf on the spray.

I wish, oh, I wish, I was yonder cloud,
That sails about with its misty shroud;
Books and work I no more should see,
And I'd come and float, dear mother, o'er thee.

Mothersense

I've heard people talk about horse sense and common sense; I've even known some who enjoy discussing nonsense, but I very rarely hear anyone address the most remarkable sense of all—Mothersense. While common sense might have logic in its corner and horse sense perhaps has experience; while nonsense might titillate us with humor, only Mothersense carries the triple punch of ethics, morality, and guilt. Mothersense doesn't have to *make* sense, it just *is* sense—for the most undeniable reason ever offered: "Because I said so!"

Mothersense doesn't dwell equally in all places, nor does it exist wholly in one location. It sort of comes and goes whither it will, visiting itself upon children of all ages. It covers a wide range of subjects and usually has something to offer on any topic.

Mothersense is always informed and up-to-date. For instance, consider "nice" people and their habits. Nice people, Mothersense reminds us, don't pick their teeth, wear dirty underwear, make rude noises in public, or spit. Nice people always say "please" and "thank you," wait their turn, and make up compliments about foods they hate. Sincerity, you see, is less important than impression on the scales of Mothersense.

Mothersense, I believe, should be a required course in medical school. There are lots of tips doctors could use. Doctors should be told, for instance, about the inexplicable link between golashes and pneumonia. They need to know about chicken soup as a cheap alternative to all those expensive cold remedies. And any devotee of Mothersense knows you stuff a cold and starve a fever. But have you ever had a doctor tell you that? No, they spend their time ferreting out things you can't even see, like viruses and bacteria. What good is that? Any mother knows that most diseases come from not listening to your mother! Why, we could probably stamp out most major diseases if people would just put their used gum in the wrapper, carry a handkerchief, and stay out of drafts—things every mother knows!

Mothersense has also made great inroads into the sciences of psychology and sociology. You want to feel good about yourself? Stand up straight, look the other person in the eye, and—for goodness' sake—speak up! Got a problem with depression? Mothers know things will look a whole lot brighter if you'll just blow your nose, splash cold water on your face, and get a grip on yourself.

Of course, Mothersense isn't limited to these fields alone. Nutrition is a big arena for the exercise of Mothersense. Eating raw cookie dough, mixing fresh cherries and milk, and avoiding spinach all bring dire consequences—anyone knows that! And no matter how much you hate something, eating a few bites each time it is served will result in the offending food becoming your favorite. Soda pop makes your face break out and rots your teeth. Ditto for chocolate, doughnuts, and ice cream. Sucking lemons will dissolve all your tooth enamel. And chewing ice will crack what the lemons leave, mark my words!

There is little doubt that Mothersense provides answers to most of life's major mysteries. It can tell you in a minute if you're "going nowhere fast," "barking up the wrong tree," or "heading for trouble, young lady!"

But Mothersense doesn't just answer questions, it asks them, too. In fact, I'd be willing to bet that the Socratic Method didn't begin with Socrates, but can be directly traced to the philosopher's mother! Do any of these leading questions sound familiar?

"Look at that door! Do you think we live in a barn?"

"Is there some reason why you can't put things back where they belong?"

"Does money grow on trees?"

"Do I look like the maid?"

Well, I'm sure you get the idea.

Whereas it's obvious that Mothersense is as ancient as humanity, I'm still puzzled about how mothers get it. I suppose it could come through the genes, somehow linked to a female chromosome. But then it might just spontaneously develop in a woman's brain shortly after the delivery of her first child. All I know is it's there and it works, and if you need a reason to believe it, try "because I said so!"

Pamela Kennedy is a freelance writer of short stories, articles, essays, and children's books. Mother of three children, she has made her home on both U. S. coasts and currently resides in Hawaii. She draws her material from her own experiences and memories, adding bits of imagination to create a story or mood.

I STILL
SEE CHILDREN

Mary Mason

Awhile ago, my little ones
Were playing at my feet.
With tiny hands clasped firm in mine,
My joy became complete.

I did not ever realize how fast
Those carefree days would go.
I seldom paused to think—
Back then, I could not know.

I saw them only yesterday
At play upon the floor.
Today they're gone; and silence marks
The closing of the door.

Now three grown men have claimed the place
Three small boys once shared,
But sometimes, in a word or look,
I still see children there.

Deana Deck

A Rose Is a Rose . . . Or Is It?

When I was about seven, I was fascinated with the roses growing in the yard next door to my grandmother's house. Some imaginative person had planted a red climber on one side of an arching latticework trellis and a white one on the opposite side. They became so intertwined that it was impossible to tell which was rooted where. My friends and I played "Sleeping Beauty," using that overgrown trellis as our castle gate. We took turns being the princess, reenacting her romantic coma in the fragrant shade cast by the enormous ancient roses.

I've been thinking about those roses recently. Today they are called old garden roses, to distinguish them from the modern hybrid varieties. I know that memory intensifies reality, but I am convinced that those roses had a fragrance that modern roses lack.

You can stand next to any hybrid rose in my garden, bury your nose in a bloom, and you will not detect a fragrance as spicy and sweet as those roses produced.

Something else I remember—or don't remember: I don't remember anyone ever spraying those roses, or pruning them, or mulching them. I don't remember them losing all their leaves to black spot every year, and I don't remember their leaves turning dusty from powdery mildew. They bloomed each spring and on into summer, seemingly requiring no special attention.

My hybrid tea roses, on the other hand, are like spoiled children. You cannot do enough for them. They demand attention, and if you do not give it to them, you will find yourself racked with guilt as the dying leaves begin to flutter to the ground.

In September I traveled to Ireland and noticed that roses were everywhere in full bloom and in full foliage. Back home, my hybrid Peace and Tropicana roses were putting out only the occasional fall bud. When I asked what variety they were, I was told they were just "old Irish roses!"

I am rapidly becoming convinced that the modern rose is not all that it is cracked up to be. Its greatest virtue seems to be the unlimited range of colors available, especially in the delicate shadings of pink, yellow, and ivory. Still, not all of these colors are to my liking. There are lavender and blue roses available now, and a depressingly dark red that is nearly black. And some of the corals are so orange they don't quite fit in with the rest of the garden. My Tropicana glows like a neon peach. When I pick it, I put it in a bud

vase on a windowsill, away from any other colors, and soften it with a sprig of baby's breath.

I have discovered something interesting about these plants: most hybrid tea roses are grafted onto the root system of a Rugosa. This is one of the toughest and most long-lived of all roses; that is why its roots are used to anchor the delicate hybrids. This makes me wonder why nurseries only sell the bottom half of the plant—the top sounds so promising!

Old garden roses are so named because their origins date earlier than 1867, the year the first hybrid teas were introduced. Today they can be ordered from nurseries with names like "Antique Rose Emporium" and "Roses of Yesterday."

I've decided that this is my year to try a couple of these old garden roses. I'm starting with a pale salmon Alfred de Dalmas, which is a moss rose of legendary scent, and a white bourbon, called Souvenir de la Malmaison—a trouble-free rose reputed to produce fragrant double blossoms throughout the season. We shall see.

If you decide to try one of these venerable beauties, purchase them in containers and plant them this fall. As with all perennials, the more time you spend preparing a planting hole, the healthier your plants will be. Dig a hole at least two feet deep and fill it with a mixture of five parts rich organic matter (compost, peat moss, dehydrated cow manure), four parts loamy garden soil, and one part builder's sand for drainage. All materials are available at your garden center.

Be sure to keep the plant well watered, especially for the first year while the roots are becoming established. You can't give a new rose too much water. Old garden roses usually require only one feeding annually, preferably in spring just before the buds begin to open. If the variety is one that blooms again in late summer, give it a second feeding with liquid fertilizer just after the first bloom period ends.

Your local garden center will be able to suggest sources for different varieties of old garden roses. Write for the catalogs, and join me in the rose revolution.

Deana Deck's garden column is a regular feature in the Tennessean. *Ms. Deck grows her roses in Nashville, Tennessee*

Story and illustration by P.K. Hallinan
from *We're Very Good Friends, My Mother and I,*
Copyright © 1989 by P.K. Hallinan.
Published by Ideals Publishing Corporation, Nashville, TN.

48

We're Very Good Friends, My Mother and I

P. K. Hallinan

We're very good friends,
My mother and I.
We like to take walks
And watch birds fly by.

And sometimes we'll just laugh
For hours on end,
But that's what you do
When you've got a true friend.

We do lots of great things,
My mother and I.
We shop at the store.
We swim at the shore.
We rest on the couch
After doing our chores.

We even cook dinners
With patience and care,
Then sit down and eat
All the treats we've prepared.

And sometimes we'll go
For a walk in the park
And swing on the swings
Till the park gets too dark.

Or sometimes we'll go
For a stroll down the lane
And make up new games
With their own special names,

Like "Hide and Seek Monster!"
Or "Catch As Catch Can!"
Or "Run Just for Fun
From the Hundred Ton Man!"

But also we're happy
Just reading good books,
Curled up in a blanket
In our own private nooks.

And, yes, we're content
Doing nothing at all,
But that's how it goes
With good friends, you know.

We have wonderful moments,
My mother and I.
Then late in the evening
As the sun's sinking low,
We'll watch the world changing,
Rearranging its glow.

And my heart feels so full
That it's bursting inside,
And I start overflowing
With gladness and pride.

My mother is special
In so many ways.
She makes me feel better
On feeling-poor days

And she eases my hurt
When I've taken a fall.
I know in my heart
She's the best mom of all!

Yes, she's taught me to care
And to never stop giving,
And she's taught me that love
Is the purpose for living.

So I guess I could never count
All the reasons why . . .
We're very good friends,
My mother and I!

49

Thoughts of
A Busy Mother

Margaret D. Nanny

If I can't find the time to wash the floor,
Who will remember or care?
If I don't patch the hole in their old blue jeans,
They can wear another pair.

The dust can sit right where it is,
For tomorrow there will be more.
If the day is too short to bake a cake,
I can always run to the store.

But if I forget to wipe a tear
Or to kiss an injured knee,
To cheer a frown, turn it upside down
Til they're chuckling with glee:

If I would fail to stop and chat
When their tales are filled with woe,
To listen for unspoken words
That only sad eyes show,

If I missed a chance to see the world
Through their precious eyes . . .
A dandelion, a crawly bug,
A rainbow in the sky,

Then I've missed a chance to share the day
With one I hold most dear;
For God was knocking at my heart
And I was too busy to hear.

GOD GAVE TO ME A CHILD

James B. Singleton

God gave to me a child—and then I knew
      The precious gift of life, the beating heart,
The little hand that clings in childish trust,
      The shining eyes that are so much a part
            Of every moment in a parent's day;
            A language that no words could ever say.

God gave to me a child—and then I knew
      The joy of love fulfilled, the quiet peace
Of home and fireside where, with strife denied,
      The heart can calmly rest in love's release,
            Can gain strength in knowing angels stand
            Around little ones with guarding hand.

God gave to me a child—and then I knew
      The parenthood of God, the eternal care
Of he who keeps the night watch and never sleeps,
      Who, when his children need him, is always there.
            I sought his kingdom for so long a while,
            And then I found it in my little baby's smile.

Photo Opposite
Innocence
Robert Cushman Hayes Photography

Happy Mother's Day

Irene Larsen

I wish you,
        Clocks that run slowly
        As the years pass by
        And music played softly
        For you to dream by.

I wish you,
    New seasons and dreams
    With your love close by;
    Starshine and moonbeams,
    Blessings from on high.

I wish you,
    All the joy a heart can hold
    With faith to lead the way;
    Wishes come true—a hundred-fold
    And a happy Mother's Day.

He Serves His Country Best

Susan Coolidge

He serves his country best
Who lives pure life and doeth righteous deed,
And walks straight paths however others stray,
And leaves his sons, as uttermost bequest,
A stainless record which all men may read;
    This is the better way.

No drop but serves the slowly lifting tide;
No dew but has an errand to some flower;
No smallest star but sheds some helpful ray,
And man by man, each helping all the rest,
Make the firm bulwark of the country's power;
    There is no better way.

Photo Opposite
Patriotism
Larry Lefever/Grant Heilman Photography, Inc.

Bits & Pieces

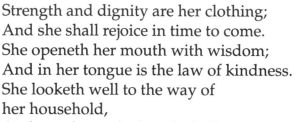

Strength and dignity are her clothing;
And she shall rejoice in time to come.
She openeth her mouth with wisdom;
And in her tongue is the law of kindness.
She looketh well to the way of
her household,
And eateth not the bread of idleness.
Her children arise up, and call her blessed;
Her husband also, and he praiseth her.
  Many daughters have done virtuously,
  But thou excellest them all.

Proverb 31:25-29

And Ruth said, Intreat me not to leave thee,
or to return from following after thee: for
whither thou goest, I will go; and where
thou lodgest, I will lodge: thy people shall be
my people, and thy God my God.

Ruth 1:16-17 to her
mother-in-law, Naomi

But I had not so much of man in me,
And all my mother came into mine eyes
And gave me up to tears.

William Shakespeare

Children are the anchors that hold a mother
to life.

Sophocles

Mother's Day Facts

The some 80 million mothers in the United States receive an average of 2.5 gifts each and close to 250 million cards each Mother's Day.

Children across the country call their mothers on Mother's Day: the holiday ranks second only to Christmas for number of calls in a single day.

According to the National Restaurant Association, only Thanksgiving brings more people to restaurants in the United States than does Mother's Day.

An estimated 20 million six-to-eleven year olds shop, with the help of their families, to find the perfect gifts for their mothers and grandmothers.

Statistics compiled by Starlette Howard

Photo Overleaf
Cascade Mountains, Washington
Ed Cooper Photo

50 YEARS AGO

The Bettmann Archive

Women line up outside a New York hosiery store to purchase newly available nylon stockings.

Synthetic Sale

One day last week flying columns of female New Yorkers stormed the hosiery counters of New York City department and specialty stores for the first big public sale of glassy, synthetic, much-publicized nylon stockings. In the words of one harassed clerk, it was a "madhouse." Elsewhere, in most of the hundreds of U.S. cities which shared the national debut, buyers were more philosophical, took their time

about snapping up the latest addition to women's full-fashioned knitted hose.

Nationally advertised brands of nylon hose stuck to their opening prices of $1.15, $1.25 & $1.35 a pair. But nylon's Manhattan appearance touched off a price war on unbranded lines. It was started by Manhattan's big Macy's department store, which quoted the hose at $1.08 and $1.27. Bloomingdale's cut to $1.04 & $1.23. By

62

Mrs. Henry C. McDuff of New York is snowed under by silk and nylon stockings collected for use in war materials.

mid-afternoon, Macy's was down to 98 cents & $1.17, but Bloomingdale's stayed one cent under its competitor. For buyers, packed five deep at some hosiery counters, it was wonderful. Limited to two pairs apiece, they almost cleaned up New York's 6,000-dozen pair allotment by closing time. For the stores, it was an all-time hosiery record with sales up 200 to 300%.

What helped the price war along was the action of Nylonmaker E. I. du Pont de Nemours & Co. in cancelling minimum wholesale prices on the hose. Warned by recent U.S. Supreme Court rulings against Ethyl Gasoline Corp. and against twelve oil companies for fixing prices, Du Pont went further. The company waived all labeling requirements and announced that from now on any stocking maker could buy nylon yarn without a license.

Welcome as this was to unlicensed manufacturers, they knew that their chances of getting much of the synthetic yarn were slim. For the big Du Pont plant at Seaford, Del., can turn out in the next twelve months only enough yarn for about 5,000,000 dozen pairs of nylon stockings—10% of the annual women's silk hose demand. A second plant, now building, will not swing into full production for a year. Discouraging, too, to hosiery makers was the possibility of nylon's becoming a war material. Last week the U. S. Army was testing the yarn for use in making parachutes, powder bags, etc.

TIME, May 27, 1940.

COLLECTOR'S CORNER

Cameos: the Sentimental Gem

Italian shell cameo, c. 1895

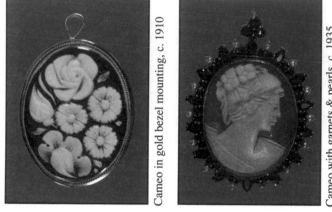

Cameo in gold bezel mounting, c. 1910

Cameo with garnets & pearls, c. 1935

For generations, the cameo has been a symbol of love and devotion, the perfect gift for special occasions in a woman's life. Favorite cameos pass from mothers to daughters to granddaughters, and become treasured heirlooms. Regardless of the whims of fashion, cameos remain popular; this one piece of jewelry appears to be everlasting.

Much is written about fashionable painters and their canvases, but we know little about great artisans of the cameo. Cameo carving developed into an industry around 400 B.C., when a vast new variety of gemstones from the East arrived in Greece. The ancient Greek cameo artists used simple hand tools supported on a spindle and spun by a bow. Cameo artists later found that a

tool made from a piece of diamond attached to an iron handle more efficiently hollowed out gems and shells.

A cameo artist first sketched an outline of the subject and then roughly scooped out the deepest parts of the relief. Careful carving revealed different colors of the shell, allowing the artist to create intricately shaded leaves, hair, and clothing.

From 1850 to 1900, the shell or coral cameo that is most familiar today was a common accessory. Cameo brooches were a part of the typical Victorian wardrobe; they were the perfect fastener for the standard high-collared bodice. The Garibaldi blouse, a loose blouse modeled after the red shirts worn by the soldiers of Garibaldi, gave rise to the success of the Italian shell cameo masters.

Cameos were available in every price range. The wealthy often had their cameos mounted in settings of gold or surrounded by precious gemstones. Many cameos were imported without mountings so that buyers could select the style and materials that best suited their needs. There was a proper cameo for every taste, and every pocketbook.

Between 1870 and 1880, the shell cameo

64

dominated women's accessories. Trimmed lace or velvet collars and ribbon neckties were worn to accent shirtwaists with high, tight bodices and the flat pin—more often than not the cameo—was a necessary pinning device.

The shell cameo was somewhat rivaled by darker mediums when carved jet cameos were seen as part of the black mourning garb adopted by Queen Victoria to signify the loss of Prince Albert.

The cameo became even more popular in the first decade of the twentieth century, when jabots of lace were pinned to the starched white linen Gibson waist, then the sensation of the fashion world.

Throughout the years, cameos have remained fashionable. Although their popularity may at times decline, they inevitably find their way back to the top of the jewel case. Worn close to the heart, the cameo symbolizes the timeless values of love and devotion as it passes on through generations of women, never losing its basic appeal.

Lillian Baker

Author, historian, and lecturer Lillian Baker has published many books on the subject of collectible jewelry and the relationship of fashion to social history. She has made public appearances, given lectures, and participated in both television and radio programs. A mother of two grown children, Mrs. Baker resides with her husband and pets in Gardena, California, where she enjoys her library and her garden.

Italian shell cameo with diamonds, c. 1875

Cameo with filigree mounting, c. 1895

Photography by Michael Kang

THE MENDING BASKET

Esther Kem Thomas

It must have been here all these years
Among the socks and thread
In my old mending basket close
Beside his little bed
Where, while I'd mend, he'd fall asleep,
But just before he "fell,"
My basket was his hideaway
For things boys love so well—
Somehow we need security
According to God's plan,
And nothing keeps things "sure and safe"
Like mending baskets can.

Today, I found one marble here
Among the mending things—
One special "shooter" warms my heart
With odd rememberings;
So careful-like he held it then—
The marble seemed to be
Too beautiful to play with
So he saved it! . . . Now to me
There's nothing can bring back those years
Of him, from child to man,
Like a long-neglected marble
In a mending basket can!

Rhododendron color show, Asheville, North Carolina   Courtesy Asheville Chamber of Commerce

A Visit to "Dixieland"

An old Victorian boardinghouse—the model for the fictional Dixieland in Thomas Wolfe's *Look Homeward, Angel*—still stands in Asheville, North Carolina, the city that inspired Wolfe's Altamont. Known as the "Old Kentucky Home" and maintained as a monument to Wolfe, the house is also a monument to the enduring appeal of Asheville. The same city that in Wolfe's day filled his mother's boardinghouse with visitors drawn by the area's beautiful mountain scenery and the distinct seasons of western North Carolina's mountain climate continues to draw tourists from all over the country. They come, as always, for the beauty of the mountains and the rejuvenation offered by the climate. But today, Asheville has even more to offer. Today, Asheville is a thriving cultural center in the midst of a still-spectacular natural setting.

Downtown Asheville has shopping and dining to suit the tastes of any visitor, including Wall Street, a cobblestone street lined with import shops and European-style restaurants, and Lexington Park, where visitors can stroll the tree-lined streets and explore the numerous antique and gift shops and the art and craft galleries along the way.

It is in Lexington Park that one will find Thomas Wolfe's "Old Kentucky Home." The house is now an official North Carolina State Historic Site and is open to the public year-round. The furnishings were arranged by surviving members of Wolfe's family to look exactly as they did at the time of the publication of *Look Homeward, Angel*, and a tour through the house takes one back in time to the early days of the twentieth century.

Those who have read the novel will find the experience especially fascinating; passages from Wolfe's text come alive inside the walls of the boardinghouse and seeing the rooms first hand impresses upon one what a profound effect the old house must have had on Wolfe's developing imagination. But even those without a knowledge of Wolfe or his work will enjoy walking through the rooms and envisioning a boardinghouse of years past, filled with earlier travelers to Asheville. Here, just as it was in the novel, is the parlor, furnished with rocking chairs where boarders could sit and rest or read in the late afternoon, or in the evening before bed. The dining room is also recreated; boarders gathered here at mealtimes to share the food that Eliza prepared daily in her own kitchen. Today, visitors can see that kitchen as it was, with the old-fashioned iron stove and Eliza's ironing board and flat irons.

Off through a side hallway sits the sun parlor. This was an evening room, a place to sit and listen to music played on the phonograph, or to the piano playing of another guest or the proprietress' children. At bedtime, boarders climbed the stairs to the bedrooms and sleeping porch on the top floors. The bedrooms remain furnished as they once were, and visitors can imagine guests of days past turning to these rooms as their homes away from home.

The exception to the restoration of the boardinghouse is a pair of rooms, one of which has been filled with a collection of Wolfe's father's personal belongings—his original furniture, his smoking stand, and his walking canes—and items from his office, including the tools he used in his downtown monument shop. Another room is a replica of one of Thomas Wolfe's New York apartments, complete with an original typewriter and a period brass lamp. Although this room is now contained by the walls of the boardinghouse, it is easy to imagine the solitude Wolfe found in New York as he turned the facts of his life into masterpieces of fiction. And yet, the room is not entirely a place of isolation; included in the restoration is the daybed that Wolfe purchased for his mother's visits to the city, and on the floor is a worn old suitcase, a reminder of the fact that this quiet New York apartment was not always home to Wolfe.

Outside the house, to the left of the entrance, is a playhouse, originally part of the house two blocks away on Woodfin Street where Thomas Wolfe was born. This is the only surviving part of Wolfe's birthplace and it was moved to the Lexington Park grounds to guarantee its survival.

The "Old Kentucky Home" is an ordinary frame house, not nearly as visually spectacular as many of the other attractions of Asheville. Yet the old house reflects a certain, significant, aspect of the the character of Asheville—a city that despite its growth to a population of over 62,000 remains a place for peaceful retreat and reflection. Asheville today offers travelers the best of both worlds: all the benefits of a modern city in a timeless natural setting.

Bedroom, Thomas Wolfe Memorial   Dawn Lankford

Kitchen, Thomas Wolfe Memorial   Nick Lanier

Sun parlor, Thomas Wolfe Memorial   Courtesy Thomas Wolfe Memorial

From *Look Homeward, Angel*, by Thomas Wolfe:

Eliza saw Altamont not as so many hills, buildings, people: she saw it in the pattern of a gigantic blueprint. She knew the history of every piece of valuable property—who bought it, who sold it, who owned it in 1893, and what it was now worth. She watched the tides of traffic cannily; she knew by what corners the largest number of people passed in a day or an hour; she was sensitive to every growing-pain of the young town, gauging from year to year its growth in any direction, and deducing the probable direction of its future expansion. She judged distance critically, saw at once where the beaten route to an important centre was stupidly circuitous, and looking in a straight line through houses and lots, she said:

"There'll be a street through here some day."

Her vision of land and population was clear, crude, focal—there was nothing technical about it: it was extraordinary for its direct intensity. Her instinct was to buy cheaply where people would come; to keep out of pockets and culs de sac, to buy on a street that moved toward a centre, and that could be given extension.

Thus, she began to think of Dixieland. It was situated five minutes from the public square, on a pleasant sloping middleclass street of small homes and boarding-houses. Dixieland was a big cheaply constructed frame house of eighteen or twenty drafty high-ceilinged rooms: it had a rambling, unplanned, gabular appearance, and was painted a dirty yellow. It had a pleasant green front yard, not deep but wide, bordered by a row of young deep-bodied maples: there was a sloping depth of one hundred and ninety feet, a frontage of one hundred and twenty. And Eliza, looking toward the town, said: "They'll put a street behind there some day."

. . . .

Thus, before he was eight, Eugene gained another roof and lost forever the tumultuous, unhappy, warm centre of his home. He had from day to day no clear idea where the day's food, shelter, and lodging was to come from, although he was reasonably sure it would be given: he ate wherever he happened to hang his hat, either at Gant's or at his mother's; occasionally, although infrequently, he slept with Luke in the sloping, alcoved, gabled back room, rude with calcimine, with the high drafty steps that slanted to the kitchen porch, with the odor of old stacked books in packing-cases, with the sweet orchard scents.

Photo Opposite
The Thomas Wolfe Memorial
Asheville, North Carolina
Steve Hill

Obscurity

Essie L. Mariner

The wild flowers have no shady room
In which to glorify their bloom,
But storms will leave them brighter hued,
And bees will seek them out for food.

Perhaps beside some flower of grace,
They hold an insignificant place;
Mayhap they grow the poor to bless,
Who love their gypsy loveliness.

Just as obscurity may be
The lot of wild flowers, you and me;
We'll do our part, for this they teach,
"There is a work God gave to each."

Photo Opposite
Moss and Monkey Flowers
Bugaboo Mountains, British Columbia
Ed Cooper Photo

Country
CHRONICLE
— Lansing Christman —

When I was a boy of thirteen, and eager to learn about wildflowers, my mother took me to Gray's Flats, a long, green spread of level ground below a waterfall, to see the trilliums in bloom. That was Mother's Day, 1923.

It was a long, creekside walk, with dozens of plants blossoming along the two or three wooded miles from our upstate New York home to the flats. We passed a large pond, one that was said to never go dry—a fisherman's paradise—but we did not leave the richly fragrant woods to inspect the bright water's surface for signs of churning fish. We were looking for flowers.

My mother, who was a botanist, identified the violets, coltsfoot, Dutchman's-breeches, bloodroot, and yellow lady-slipper along the way. The herb Robert, jack-in-the-pulpit, pale corydalis, and unfolding ferns bordered the woodside. In more secluded parts of the woods, wild pinxter thrived, sweet and rich with spring.

When we arrived at Gray's Flats, the terrain shimmered with the fresh breezes and fragrances

which only gentle May can nurture out of the earth and air. Before us were the verdant flats, surrounded by thick woods and closed in on two sides by steep hills, one of which climbed sharply to a higher plateau of meadows, fields, and pastures.

The rich soil held the large-flowered trilliums in masses along the bordering woods. Each held a whorl of three leaves from the center of which rose a single, three-petalled blossom. I learned that they are part of the lily family; I did not have to be taught to appreciate their delicate beauty. In the cool, loamy shelter, the trilliums spread graciously over last winter's leaves like courtly ladies in mid-curtsy.

That long-ago Mother's Day may well have been the spark which kindled my life-long interest in wildflowers. I have since walked many miles through woods, pastures, fields, and marshes, admiring the beauty unfolding around me from season to season.

I remember vividly that May day in 1923, when my mother took me on my first venture into the loveliness of the world of flowers. That special day, the trilliums painted the woodland white, as clean and pure as newly fallen snow, as though honoring the purity of a mother's love.

The author of two published books, Lansing Christman has been contributing to Ideals for almost twenty years. Mr. Christman has also been published in several American, foreign, and braille anthologies. He and his wife, Lucile, live in rural South Carolina where they enjoy the pleasures of the land around them.

Photo Overleaf
Cape Hatteras Lighthouse
North Carolina
Ken Dequaine Photography

AMERICANA
THE MONTH OF MAY

Alice B. Dorland

The day is sparkling, blue and gold,
The time, the end of the month of May.
We've packed our tackle and oldest clothes
For we're off on a fishing holiday.

These are the sights that meet the eye,
A country fresh from April rain,
Apple trees all pink with bloom,
Vivid tulips in flower again.

Here is a man with a burning torch
For tent caterpillars in his fruit trees,
Another man's mending his cow shed roof,
Here laundry blows in the breeze.

There are shadows of clouds on distant hills,
Brooks that we pass are filled to the brim,
In a barnyard pond that mirrors the skies
Brown ducks swim.

Someone is painting her porch chairs green,
Someone has winter clothes to air,
White geese are arguing down by the stream
An old man is plowing behind his gray mare.

A painted tire upon a front lawn
Has its center planted with pansies gay,

Now we bring our car to a sudden stop
As a woodchuck crosses our way.

A cow rubs her neck on the trunk of a tree,
A red-winged blackbird flashes by,
And now and again we hear far away
The white, crowned sparrow's insistent cry.

There are polished tins of geraniums growing
In many a window as we pass,
In a churchyard women are planting bright flowers,
An old man is cutting the holiday grass.

These are the sights that warm our hearts,
America along the way.
Her golden sunshine and clear, blue skies
Are never so fair as they are in May.

Readers' Forum

I love your Ideals magazine . . . and I use it for my Recreation and Park Department Therapeutic Recreation Program for disabled children. They love to listen to all those wonderful stories and poems. It really touches their special needs. Me too! Thanks for this beautiful magazine.

Karen L. Wills
Thousand Oaks, California

I have been receiving your magazine about two years. It never fails to help me. In the Country Ideals, Alice B. Dorland brought back memories of when I was a girl on the farm . . . The Ideals is soul inspiring, also. I really enjoy it very much.

Mrs. Margaret Mumea
Galion, Ohio

Two years ago I moved from my hometown, Lawrenceville, Georgia, to Nashville, Tennessee. Moving was a very hard situation for my mother and myself . . . One day I received a copy of Ideals in the mail from my mother with a note saying she had purchased a year's subscription for me. In doing this, she has given me a gift that we continuously share over the phone, in letters to each other, and with friends and family . . . Thank you for making our separation easier and more of a joy when we do get to talk to or see each other.

Michelle Kemp Roberson
Nashville, Tennessee

I just had to let you know how very much I enjoy your publication. I look forward to receiving each issue. . . Since I love to travel, but don't get the opportunity to very often, I feel as though I'm visiting other parts of our great country through your wonderful photographs.

Sandy Sample
Edinburg, Illinois

Thank you for allowing me to recapture a sense of serenity and calmness through the pages of your lovely magazine. Reading each page aloud recaptures the values and traditions that the larger society seemingly has abandoned.

Hattie M. Suber
Newport News, Virginia

I look forward to each edition of Ideals. It is such a beautiful book and the poems are so inspiring. I live in an apartment for the elderly and read your poems often at gatherings.

Evelyn Gering
Louisville, Kentucky

* * *

Ed: Several readers wrote to point out an error in our 1989 Home issue. The St. Paul Como Conservatory pictured on page 5 is located in St. Paul, Minnesota, and not, as noted in the caption, St. Paul, Missouri. We thank our readers for bringing this to our attention, and we apologize for our mistake.

* **Want to share your crafts?**
Readers are invited to submit original craft ideas for possible development and publication in future Ideals issues. Please send query letter (with photograph, if possible) to Editorial Features Department, Ideals Publishing Corporation, P.O. Box 140300, Nashville, Tennessee 37214-0300. Please do not send craft samples; they cannot be returned.

ideals
Celebrating Life's Most Treasured Moments

"Mother and Child" by Mary Cassatt
Globe Photos